Take Me Out to the
BALL GAME

A Trip to a
MAJOR LEAGUE
BASEBALL
GAME

★ ★ ★

by Andra Serlin Abramson

APPLESAUCE · PRESS

Kennebunkport, Maine

For Jordan, a Phillies fan
–ASA

13-Digit ISBN: 978-1-60433-060-1
10-Digit ISBN: 1-60433-060-0

This book may be ordered by mail from the publisher. Please include $2.50 for postage and handling.
Please support your local bookseller first!

Books published by Applesauce Press and Cider Mill Press Book Publishers are available at special discounts for bulk purchases in the United States by corporations, institutions, and other organizations.
For more information, please contact the publisher.

Cider Mill Press Book Publishers
"Where good books are ready for press"
12 Port Farm Road
Kennebunkport, Maine 04046

Visit us on the Web!
www.cidermillpress.com

Design and layout by T. Reitzle / Oxygen Design
Printed in China

1 2 3 4 5 6 7 8 9 0
First Edition

Library of Congress Control Number: 2008911342

Contents

Let's Go to the Game!

Here we are at the stadium. On game day, the flags are flying and excitement is in the air.

LET'S GO TO A BASEBALL GAME! Whether this is your first trip to a Major League game or your 100th, it will be an exciting time from the first inning to the ninth. Come on and pick up your ticket at the booth and let's go in to the stadium. The game is about to begin and we have lots to see!

Let's head to the ticket booth to pick up our tickets. Can't wait to see where we are sitting.

Did You Know...

Americans have been playing baseball for more than a century. Originally people played on small ball fields with just a few hundred fans to watch the action. But today Major League Baseball is played in huge stadiums with tens of thousands of fans watching at a time.

Baseball Basics

BATTING AVERAGE:
The number of hits a player has, divided by the number of at bats.

Look overhead.
There's the Goodyear Blimp. For more than 75 years, the Blimp has made appearances over sporting events like Major League Baseball games.

Time to head through the turnstiles with thousands of other baseball fans. It won't be long before the game begins.

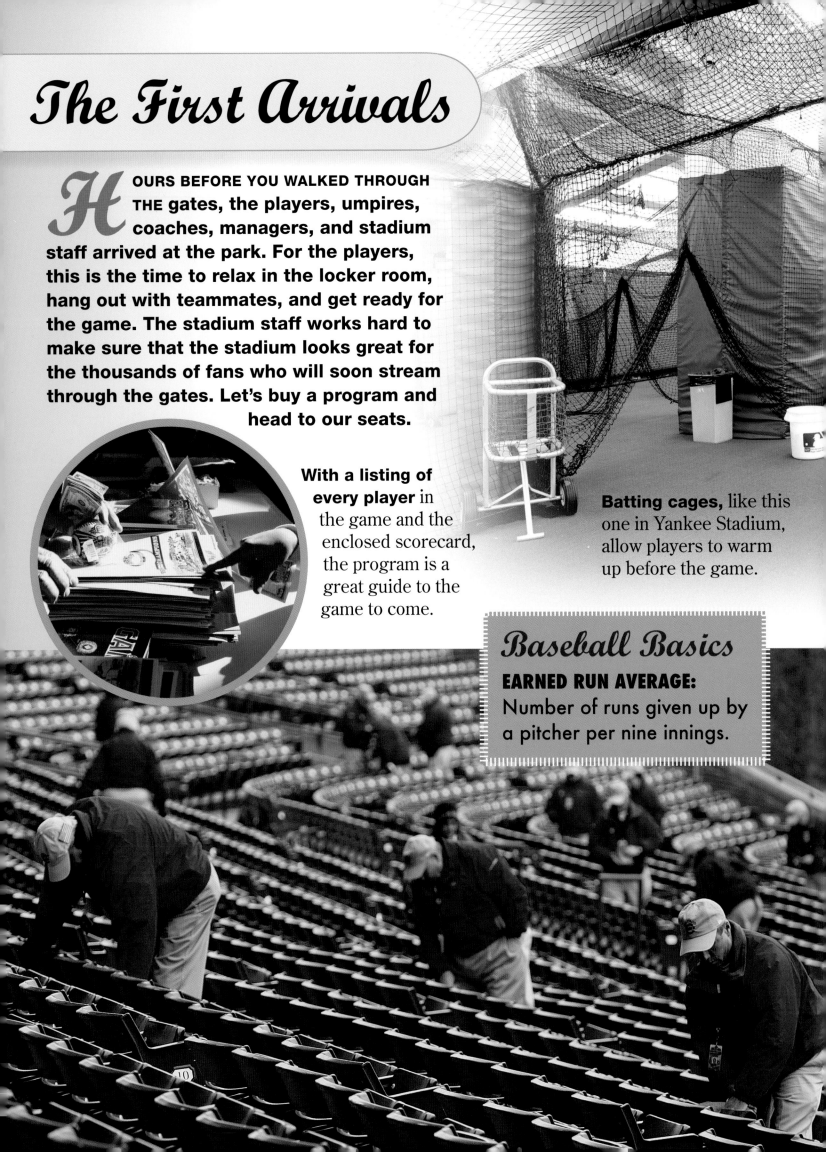

The First Arrivals

HOURS BEFORE YOU WALKED THROUGH THE gates, the players, umpires, coaches, managers, and stadium staff arrived at the park. For the players, this is the time to relax in the locker room, hang out with teammates, and get ready for the game. The stadium staff works hard to make sure that the stadium looks great for the thousands of fans who will soon stream through the gates. Let's buy a program and head to our seats.

With a listing of every player in the game and the enclosed scorecard, the program is a great guide to the game to come.

Batting cages, like this one in Yankee Stadium, allow players to warm up before the game.

Baseball Basics

EARNED RUN AVERAGE: Number of runs given up by a pitcher per nine innings.

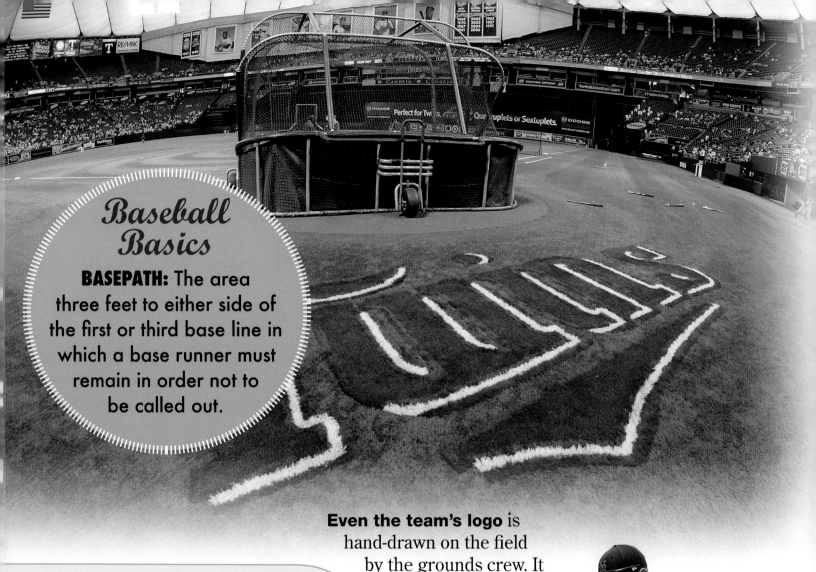

Even the team's logo is hand-drawn on the field by the grounds crew. It takes dozens of people to maintain the field to the high standards players and fans expect.

Get a Look at that Field!

WOW, GET A LOOK AT THAT FIELD! A professional baseball field can be a pretty amazing sight. From the freshly cut turf to the perfectly straight foul lines, every inch of the field is groomed to provide the best playing experience possible. The groundskeepers work hard to make sure every fan who steps out of the tunnel feels a sense of awe when they first see the field. These are great seats aren't they? Even though the stadium can hold thousands of people, it is built so that everyone feels like they are part of the action.

Prior to the game, the dirt is watered down to help keep dust from getting in the players' eyes.

With its contrasting colors of green and white, the baseball diamond practically glows under the sun (or under the lights during a night game).

Did You Know...

Did You Know...

Although you may not notice it, high above the field preparations are being made in the broadcast booth. From here, each and every play will be called and the game will be broadcast to millions of viewers around the world. It's the broadcaster's job to help fans watching the game at home understand what they are seeing. The stadium announcer is the voice you hear in the ball park.

Before every game, ushers wipe off all the seats in the stadium to make sure they are clean and dry.

The locker room is a great place for the players to unwind before and after the game. Hanging out together helps players work better as a team.

The Dugout and Bullpen

LOOK DOWN THERE. Do you see the dugout? That's where the players are gathering for their final instructions before the start of the game. All the equipment they will need to play safely is stored in the dugout, including bats, batting helmets, gloves, and first aid equipment. Nearby, in the bullpen, the pitcher is warming up his muscles. As in any sport, baseball players must be in peak condition to perform at the top of their game.

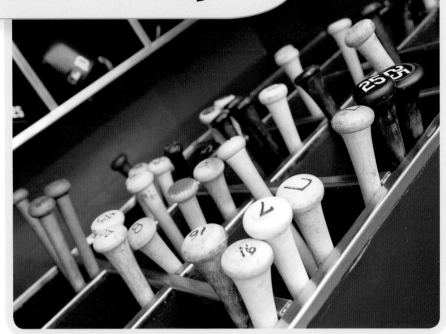

Bats, helmets, mitts, and other equipment are neatly stored in the dugout so that each player can quickly and easily find his equipment when it is needed.

Baseball Basics

DESIGNATED HITTER: A player who is allowed to bat for the pitcher in the American League.

Each team has a dugout located on either the first base or third base line. From the dugout, players can see everything that happens on the field.

To get the home plate box exactly right, the groundskeepers use an oversized stencil to make sure the lines are correct.

Did You Know?

Baseball stadiums may look different, but the baseball diamond is pretty standard. It is 60 feet 6 inches from the pitchers mound to the back corner of home plate and 90 feet between first base and second. To hit a home run a player must hit the ball at least 302 feet up the foul line to as much as 435 feet at center field.

Here's the view from our seats. From here we'll be close enough to catch any fly balls that come our way. Better keep your mitt handy!

Before the game the players take turns stretching their muscles and warming up on the field. It's a great chance for the players on different teams to get to know each other.

Did You Know...

When a Major League Baseball pitcher warms up in the bullpen, it isn't the regular team catcher warming up with him. Instead, the team has a warm up catcher. His job is to work with the pitcher in the bullpen, helping him get ready to do his best.

The bullpen, where the pitchers warm up, is often located in the back of the field behind where a homerun would go.

Baseball Basics

WORLD SERIES: The championship series of Major League Baseball.

Get Your Peanuts and Popcorn Here

Working the stands high above the game is a thrill only a few people will ever experience. It can be hard work, but it's fun, too.

NOW THAT WE'RE IN OUR SEATS, you are probably ready for one of the best traditions of Major League Baseball: peanuts, popcorn, and, of course, a hot dog. You won't even have to leave your seat to get one of these ballpark treats, they'll come to you by way of one of the hardworking strolling vendors who roam the stadium.

Hope you're hungry! If so, head out to the concession stands to pick up a hotdog with the works!

16

Did You Know...

A common treat at baseball games for more than a century is Cracker Jack, molasses covered peanuts and popcorn. Cracker Jack was created in 1896 and has been a fan favorite ever since. The line "Buy me some peanuts and Cracker Jack" in the song "Take Me Out to the Ballgame," written in 1908, shows how entwined the sweet treat has become with the game of baseball.

Even the mascot can't resist having a treat at the game.

Concession row at many stadiums has a wide variety of food choices to please every tastebud.

proudly we hailed at the twilight's last gleaming?

JANUARY 1
2009

St. Petersburg Times

State

WELCOME TO TROPICANA FIELD

While the National Anthem is playing and the flag is being displayed, everyone is on the same team. No matter which team you are rooting for, this is the time to remember that we are all Americans.

The National Anthem

IT'S TIME TO RISE for the National Anthem. Take off your hat and stand straight and tall. As the music begins to play and "The Star Spangled Banner" blasts from the speakers, it's a great time to think about all those who have sacrificed for our freedom. Raise your voice to honor your country and your fellow citizens!

The people who escort the flag onto the field are called the "Color Guard."

Baseball Basics

WILD CARD: A team allowed to compete in the Division Championship Series without winning a division title because it has the best win-loss record of any of the remaining teams in the league.

Players from both teams line up on the baseline to honor our country's flag.

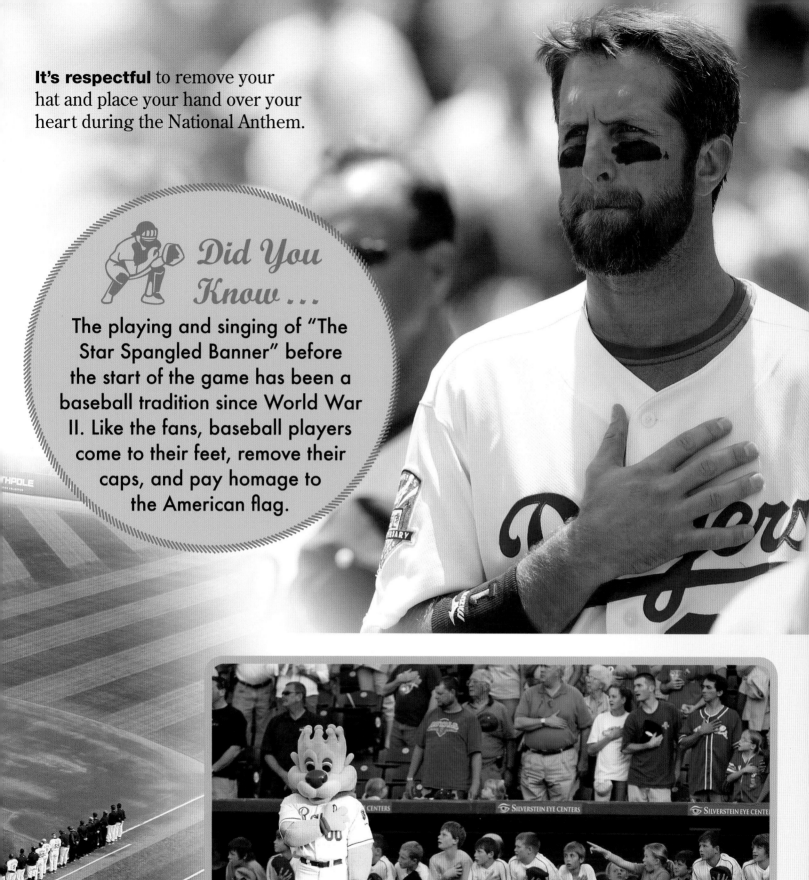

It's respectful to remove your hat and place your hand over your heart during the National Anthem.

Did You Know...

The playing and singing of "The Star Spangled Banner" before the start of the game has been a baseball tradition since World War II. Like the fans, baseball players come to their feet, remove their caps, and pay homage to the American flag.

Even the mascot comes out to salute the flag.

Batter Up!

ONCE THE FINAL NOTES of the National Anthem fade away, the umpire calls, "Batter up!" and the game begins. Get out your program and open it up to the scorecard. Here you'll find a listing of every member of both teams. It's fun to keep track of how each player does by marking his performance on the scorecard. Years later, this card will be a memento of your day at the ballpark.

The home plate umpire is responsible for calling all the balls and strikes.

The catcher uses signals to communicate with the pitcher and the rest of the team.

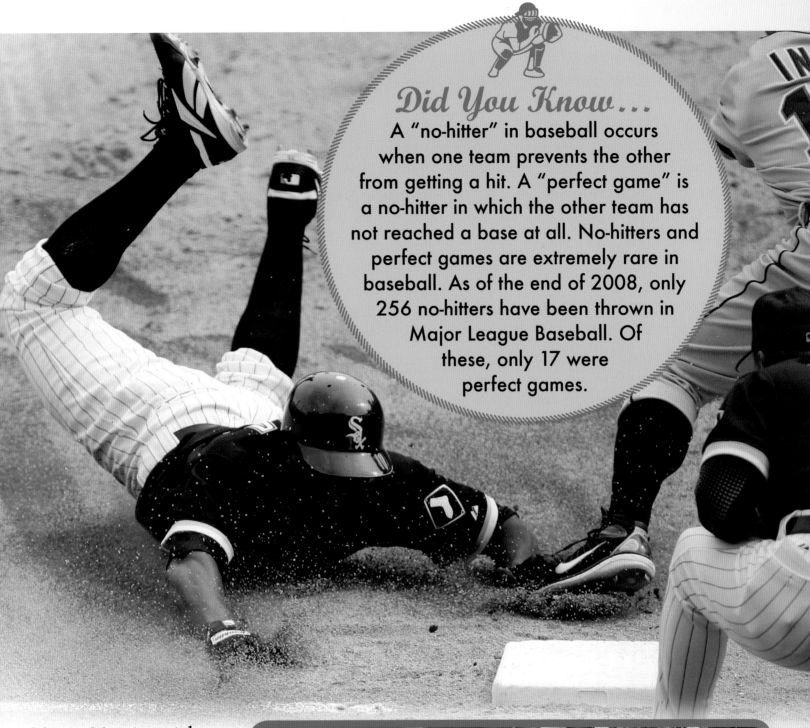

Did You Know...

A "no-hitter" in baseball occurs when one team prevents the other from getting a hit. A "perfect game" is a no-hitter in which the other team has not reached a base at all. No-hitters and perfect games are extremely rare in baseball. As of the end of 2008, only 256 no-hitters have been thrown in Major League Baseball. Of these, only 17 were perfect games.

It's exciting to watch players try to steal second base.

Baseball Basics

BASEBALL COMMISSIONER: The head administrator of professional baseball, selected for a four-year term.

Keep your glove handy. You never know when you'll be able to catch a fly ball.

Even the players get in on the fun when the mascot is around.

Like the mascots on other teams, Mr. Met, the mascot for the NY Mets, makes appearances both inside and outside the ballpark.

Hooray for the Mascot

THE FIRST INNING IS OVER and something big and furry charges onto the field. The team mascot has the important job of revving up the crowd and getting them psyched to cheer on the home team. You never know what that funny mascot is going to do next so you'll want to keep an eye on him. Wave your arms and shout, "Goooo team!"

Baseball Basics

INNING: One of the nine divisions of a baseball game in which each team is allowed to bat until they make three outs.

Dancing, playing tricks, and rooting on their team is all part of a day's work to a team mascot.

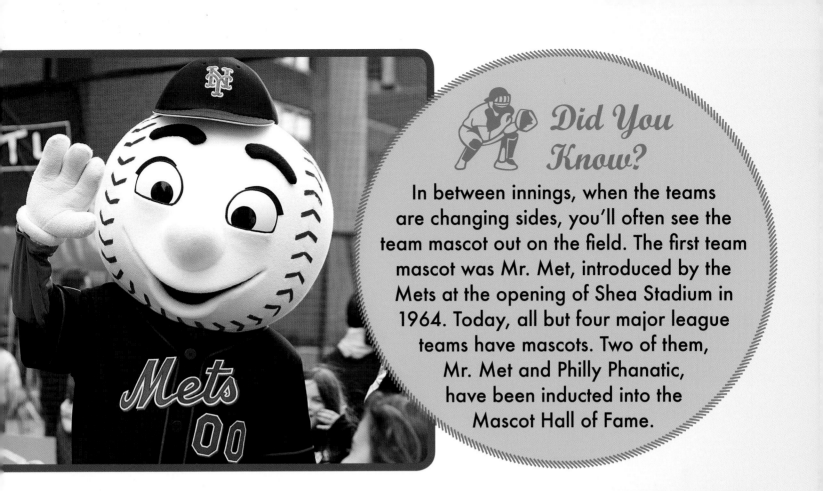

Did You Know?

In between innings, when the teams are changing sides, you'll often see the team mascot out on the field. The first team mascot was Mr. Met, introduced by the Mets at the opening of Shea Stadium in 1964. Today, all but four major league teams have mascots. Two of them, Mr. Met and Philly Phanatic, have been inducted into the Mascot Hall of Fame.

They may be funny-looking, but mascots really help the crowd rally around their team.

It takes more than a dozen strong people to put the rain cover on a field, but it's the best way to protect the playing surface the ground crew has worked so hard to get just right.

True fans don't leave the game when it rains. They put on their team ponchos and wait for the rain to stop.

Get Out Your Umbrella!

SPLISH, SPLISH, SPLASH. Raindrops are starting to come down. As we open our umbrellas, the field crew runs out to start covering the field. It takes more than a dozen strong people to roll out the tarps needed to protect the field. Don't worry, it won't be long until the rain stops. When it does, they will uncover the field and the game will get underway again.

It takes a lot of work to get the rain tarp rolled up and off the field. Give the grounds crew a round of applause for all their effort.

A rainbow is a beautiful way to end a rain delay.

Before the tarp can be removed, most of the water must be taken off of it.

The 7ᵗʰ Inning Stretch

*I*T'S THE MIDDLE OF THE 7ᵀᴴ INNING and you're in for a treat. The 7ᵗʰ Inning Stretch is a time to stand up and sing "Take Me Out to the Ballgame." It's also a time for the relief pitcher to take over, and for the teams to think about their final strategies. There's the mascot again. You never know what he might be up to during the 7ᵗʰ Inning Stretch.

Sometimes famous singers, like Vanessa Williams, come out to sing "God Bless America" during the 7th Inning Stretch.

Baseball Basics

RUNS BATTED IN (RBI): A statistic used to credit a batter when the outcome of his at-bat results in a run being scored, except in certain situations such as when an error is made on the play.

The ground crew does the "YMCA" dance while they spruce up the field.

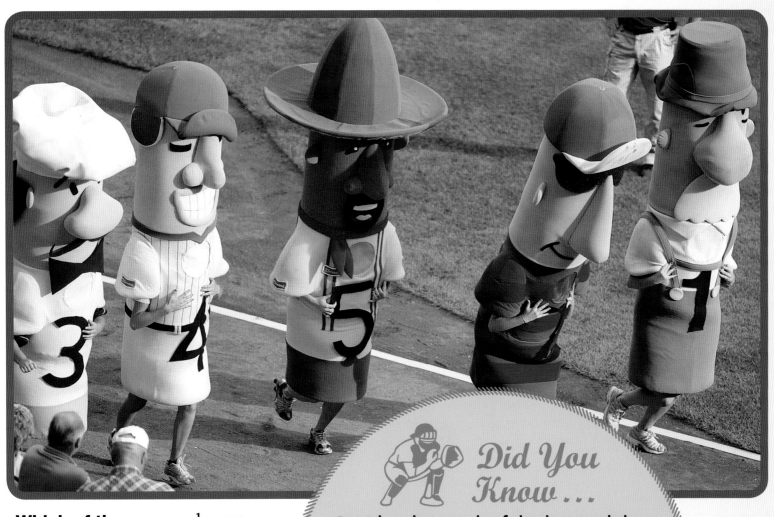

Which of these guys do you think will win the race? It's the kind of thing that only happens during the 7th Inning Stretch.

The organist is playing "Take Me Out to the Ballgame." Let's sing!

Time To Go Home

IT'S THE BOTTOM OF THE NINTH and there are two outs. The batter comes up to the plate. The pitcher throws the ball. The batter swings and hits one straight to the first baseman. He grabs the ball and touches the base. "Batter is out!" calls the umpire and the game is over. Like all good sportsmen, the teams come together on the field to congratulate each other on a game well played. They'll meet again soon for a rematch.

Now it's time for you to head home after an afternoon of fun at the game. We hope you'll come back again soon for another dose of baseball: the great American pastime.

The scoreboard at Fenway Park is the last one where the score needs to be changed by hand.

Baseball Basics

INFIELD: The part of the field located closest to the bases.

The players congratulate each other on a game well played.

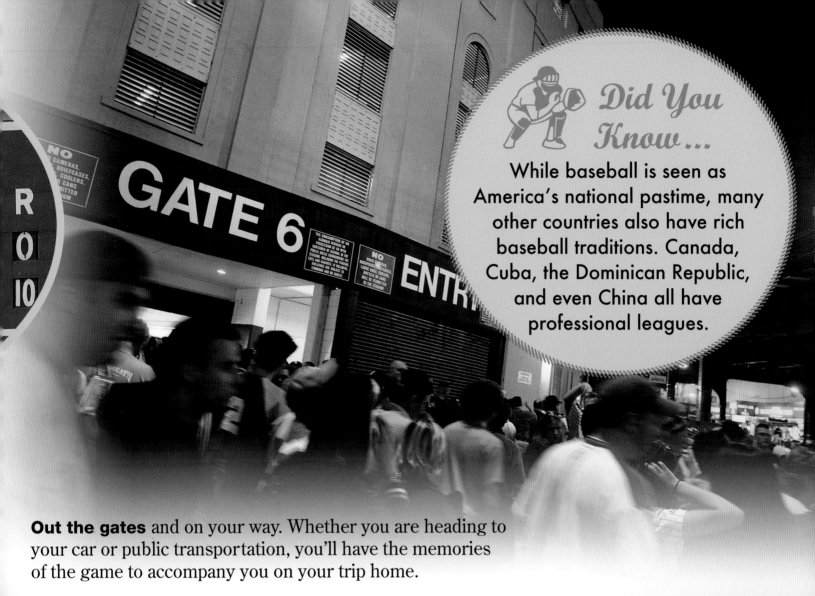

Did You Know...

While baseball is seen as America's national pastime, many other countries also have rich baseball traditions. Canada, Cuba, the Dominican Republic, and even China all have professional leagues.

Out the gates and on your way. Whether you are heading to your car or public transportation, you'll have the memories of the game to accompany you on your trip home.

Sometimes the stadium treats fans to a fireworks display after the game.

About Applesauce Press

What kid doesn't love Applesauce!

Applesauce Press was created to press out the best children's books found anywhere. Like our parent company, Cider Mill Press Book Publishers, we strive to bring fine reading, information, and entertainment to kids of all ages. Between the covers of our creatively crafted books, you'll find beautiful designs, creative formats, and most of all, kid-friendly information on pressing [important] topics. Our Cider Mill bears fruit twice a year, publishing a new crop of titles each spring and fall.

"Where Good Books are Ready for Press"

Visit us on the Web at
www.cidermillpress.com
or write to us at
12 Port Farm Road
Kennebunkport, Maine 04046

Photo Credits